Countdown to Christmas

Michelle Lores

Printed in the United States of America

ISBN: Softcover   978-1-63871-419-4
        eBook   978-1-63871-420-0

Republished by: PageTurner Press and Media LLC
Publication Date: 11 August 2021

To order copies of this book, contact:

PageTurner Press and Media
Phone: 1-888-447-9651
info@pageturner.us
www.pageturner.us

Countdown To Christmas!

*Stories, Poems, and Songs For
the 25 Days of Christmas*

Michelle Lores

Table of Contents

Countdown To Christmas!

Stories, Poems, and Songs For
the 25 Days of Christmas

Day 1:

Cody's Bear

Cody sat staring longingly out of one of the windows in the home where he lived. He longed for many things. He longed for a true home. He longed for a family. He longed to belong.

For as long as he could remember, Cody had felt cold inside and like a giant piece of him was missing.

There was just this giant hole that he couldn't seem to find a way to fill.

Cody had never really known his real mom or dad. He had been surrendered to the state as a very young child, and he could not remember ever knowing either one of them.

Cody was eight years old now and losing hope fast of ever knowing real acceptance and a father's love or a mother's tender touch. His eyes had lost their sparkle, and he was fading fast.

The home where Cody lived housed many other children in similar situations as Cody's. Cody was quiet and withdrawn and generally well-behaved, so unfortunately, the home's caretaker, Miss Julia, often overlooked him. Cody did not require much attention to be kept in line, therefore, because of the enormous demands on her time with the other children, that meant that Cody did not receive hardly any attention at all—especially not the positive kind.

But there was Someone who had not forgotten about Cody. That Someone was God Himself—Cody's Creator and the only true Heavenly Father.

You see, Cody was not ever really alone—he just did not know that yet. But, as is always the case, God had a plan in mind, and He was working it out in His ever perfect timing.

One morning when Cody was feeling especially lonely, he woke up, got dressed, and headed to the breakfast table expecting to see Miss Julia in the kitchen, as was always the case. However, he was met with a surprise. A man named Mr. Wen was waiting there instead.

"You must be Cody!" Mr. Wen said with a big smile on his face and a special twinkle in his eye.

"Well, yes… I am," Cody said strangely. He was confused. Where were the other kids? And where was Miss Julia?

"I bet you are wondering where the kids are and where Miss Julia is. Am I right, Cody?" Mr. Wen asked. "Don't worry. They are quite safe. My name is Mr. Wen, and Miss Julia is gone for the day. The other children have gone on to school, and I am here to care especially for you," Mr. Wen said with the kindest smile that Cody had ever seen.

Mr. Wen went on to cook and prepare the best breakfast that Cody had ever had. There was fruit and eggs and bacon and hash browns with ketchup and biscuits and chocolate chip pancakes and sausage and orange juice and chocolate milk! Young Cody ate some of everything until he was completely satisfied. It was heavenly!

And the whole time that Mr. Wen was preparing the food and Cody was eating it, Mr. Wen was asking Cody questions. He asked about what he liked and whathe dreamed of and who he wanted to be. He asked about his favorite color, his favorite food, and his favorite movie. He asked why Cody liked all of these things.

Cody couldn't believe that someone actually cared that much about him. No one had ever taken the time to show an interest in him before. Could this be real? How long would Mr. Wen be around? What a beautiful morning!

After breakfast, Mr. Wen played some games with Cody. They had so much fun together, and Cody wanted this time to last forever.

When the evening came, the day had been so full of fun at the home that Cody felt like it had been three days instead of one. He just loved Mr. Wen, and he knew that if he could, he would spend the rest of his days with him. Mr. Wen cared about him. No one ever had before.

Just before it was time for Mr. Wen to leave, he pulled out a little teddy bear from nowhere and said, "Cody, this bear is for you. I want you to remember something, even if you forget about me. There is Someone who cares about you. That Someone sent me to you today to care for you. He is your Heavenly Father and His Son's name is Jesus.

"God sent His only Son, Jesus, to earth to die and rise from the dead so that you could know God as your own Heavenly Father and so that you would never have to be alone again.

"You see, we all do bad things called sin. The Bible says that the bad things we do make us all deserving of eternal death and separation from God. But God loved us so much that He made a way for us to come to Him as our very own loving Father who cares very much for us—more than any earthly mom or dad ever could.

"My dear Cody. I have been sent to tell you that God loves you very much, and He desires for you to be his child. Accept Jesus as God's Son and as the One who can save you from your sins, and choose to follow Him with your whole heart, mind, and soul. Give yourself to

Him fully. You will always be able to talk to Him, and He will always be with you. Read your Bible, Cody—the one Miss Julia gave you for Christmas. You are not alone. You have never been alone, and you will never be alone.

"This little bear I am giving you is to remind you to pray to the One who is always with you. Hug this bear when you feel lonely and remember: You are Never alone.

"Good night, Dear Cody! Sweet Dreams!" Mr.

Wen gave Cody a warm hug that Cody felt all the way to the center of his cold insides, and then there was a bright flash of light and Mr. Wen was gone!

All of a sudden, Cody woke up and sat up straight in bed in the room that he shared with five other children.

It had all been a dream!

But wait! Cody felt something next to him in hisbed. It was a soft little bear with a strange expression on its face. It looked forlorn and like it needed a hug.

Cody remembered then what Mr. Wen had said in his dream: Jesus was with him.

Cody bowed his head right there in his bed, because he knew that he had to talk to the One who had given him such a special dream and such a wonderful gift.

There WAS Someone who cared about him. He wanted Jesus to be his Savior, and his Lord, and his forever Best Friend. So Cody asked God to forgive him for doing the bad things he had done and for not believing in Jesus before, and he told God that he wanted Him to help him live for Jesus every day.

He told God that he was really lonely and that he wanted to belong to a family. He asked God to be his Father and Jesus to be his very best friend. Then he thanked God for the dream and for the little forlorn bear that would remind him every day when he hugged it that God was hugging him too.

When Cody went back to sleep, he knew that he would never again be alone. And even if he fought with feelings of isolation, despair and loneliness, Cody knew beyond the shadow of a doubt that God was with him, God would never leave him, and God would never desert him.

Cody belonged to Someone now, and he couldn't wait to meet his new family—others who believe in Jesus—the church. He would read His Bible to hear

Jesus' Words and to be near Him. And with the help of God's Spirit who now lived inside of Cody, he would live to love Jesus and love others every day.

Young Cody had a purpose now. He would live to love God and to love others. And he would share this good news of God's acceptance, forgiveness, and love with the people in his life.

As the days went on, Cody experienced new life. The big hole inside of him had been filled with the Holy Spirit and God's love. Cody's days were still hard, but Cody had Someone with him now.

When he had a problem of any kind, he just went with it in prayer to Jesus and His Heavenly Father. The problem was not always solved in the way he wished, but he trusted his Lord with it.

The Bible says that God is in control, He works all things for our good—to make us more like Jesus— and we can trust Him, for God is good at ALL times.

Cody believed those words, and God's truth gave Him peace as He believed it and acted on it. Cody's action was produced by his belief in God's truth. That is called faith.

Cody grew up strong in the Lord. He never had an earthly mother or father, but God was his Father, and Jesus was his Best Friend. He became a good member of his church and community and he lived to serve the Lord and others with his life.

God saw him through much hurt and pain and ups and downs, and God never failed him, even when Cody slipped up and failed.

Cody still has his little bear from that night so long ago, and to this day, no one can explain where it came from or how it ended up in his arms that night.

But Cody knows.

God gave him the bear, just like God gave him the dream that changed his life.

God cares about the lost, the afflicted, the hurting, the oppressed, and those who are all alone. God will not leave them as orphans who come to Him. That night, God reached out to Cody, Cody responded, and now Cody has love, and he belongs to the family of the God of the universe who is now his Heavenly Father.

Life on this earth will never be easy. But that's okay, because one day, Cody will live forever in heaven with Jesus, and THEN, everything will finally be okay.

Oh, that glorious day!

When Jesus will come

And wipe every tear away!

Oh, that glorious day!

So the hearts of those who love Jesus sing,

"Come Lord Jesus,

Be our King!

Take your place and reign forever, we sing!

Come, Lord Jesus, make all things new!

So we can live and breathe freely

In heaven with You!

Until then, we will live here in joy

And embrace your peace in our hearts

And resist satan's ploy.

We will draw near to

You In life and in love

For You are true,

Full of compassion from above.

Lord, there is none like You!

This we do declare.

For Your Word is ALL true.

You are just, holy, righteous, and fair.

Lord, we love You,

And we give You our lives.

Be our Rescue—

We know You hear our cries.

Our lives belong to You now,

You are our only true hope.

You are our Home.

Wash us clean with Heavenly soap.

We want to be ready

When You come again.

We know You will never leave us.

Thank You for washing away our sin.

Jesus, be glorified

In our lives this very day.

We will worship You with a joyful heart,

Knowing that with us You will always stay."

And all of God's adopted children say,

Children, women, and men,

Now and Always,

"In Jesus' Name, Amen."

Day 2:

The Special Treasure

One night long ago, when it was snowing so hard, a family moved to a new country and a new life. They moved under the cover of darkness for fear of being seen. But they put their trust in their Creator to protect them from the dangers of the night.

Stealthily they crossed the border, each carrying all they had in a bag on their back. The two adults and two oldest children carried one more thing, too. It was luggage filled with a secret treasure that was forbidden in this new country. This family felt led to share their treasure with the people here, and so they quietly and secretly crept over the unguarded part of the border and made their way into a new country—their new home—and the people who awaited them there.

The family assumed a new identity and began to live a new life. They lived to make connections with the people they interacted with every day.

They wanted to share as much of their treasure with this new people as possible before their time in this country ran out.

Christmas time was approaching, and the family had very little, but Dad took time to chop some wood and create a beautiful nativity to put inside the house. It was simple yet complete with stable, manger, Mary, Joseph, and baby Jesus.

The best part about the nativity was that the figurines were the height of their 11 year old daughter-- they were close to life-size! And baby Jesus was the size of a real newborn baby! Their youngest daughter, Anna, loved to take the baby Jesus from his manger and hold him in her arms. She loved to look into his sweet and loving face and imagine what it would have been like to hold the real baby Jesus.

This manger scene was all the family had for Christmas, but it was enough.

They had their new friends over to their house at Christmas for hot tea, fresh baked bread, conversation around the nativity scene, and an invitation to accept their special treasure.

Dad was eventually arrested by officials in the country's government and tortured for sharing the forbidden treasure with the people. He had been betrayed by one with whom he had shared.

It was then, at the beginning of the New Year, that the family's time in the country ran out. This time, they were personally escorted across the border and out of the country.

Dad did not regret the pain he had endured to share the family's treasure. Instead, he and the family looked ahead to the next country they would go to where they would continue to share their treasure with more people in need.

~~

What was this treasure

They risked so much to give?

It is the Word of God, the Bible.

To this family, it was worth the lives they lived.

They sacrificed every comfort

To get it into others' hands.

They knew they would have an eternal reward

And that God would help them strongly stand.

Would you give your life

For Jesus and God's Word?

Or do you think that sounds ridiculous

And perhaps a bit absurd?

Even if you don't go

Into a foreign land,

You are still called to give your life for Jesus

By walking in step with Him, hand in hand.

That is what God's children

Are called to do.

To give Him everything

And live for Him, too.

Whatever He says,

Wherever He leads,

That is where we go.

Submission is the key.

May our lives be about Jesus

Wherever we may be.

Oh, He loves us so very much!

May we be His vessels of Light for all to see!

In Jesus' Name, Amen.

~Mark 8:34-38~

Day 3:

Never Alone

"It's seventy-five degrees out there, Orlando, with two days left until Christmas. Merry Christmas toall of you last minute shoppers! And don't forget to remember those who need a little extra love this Christmas! Now for more music from your station, 'The Positive Hits that Roll'!"

Janie switched off the station. She just wasn't feeling the Christmas spirit this year. She felt alone and like a Christmas grump. Janie was in her thirties, but she wasn't married. She didn't have any kids, either. This year would come like any other—she would go to her parents' house, see her brother and his happy family, exchange gifts, then go back home—alone.

Well, at least she had her cat, P.C.. P.C. stood for "Prince Charming," but he was pretty much of a loner— so much for the Charming part!

Janie had left all of her Christmas shopping this year to the day before Christmas Eve—after all, if she had left it until Christmas

Eve, that would be cutting it too close!

Janie was kept so busy with her job that she barely had time to shop at all. She was thanking God now for this time off before Christmas Eve, all the while wondering why everyone else in the world had to be on the road at the same time that she needed to get her shopping done.

Janie drove to her mom's favorite store after striking out in her search for a gift for her mom at the mall. Everyone else on her list was covered after she had found last minute purchases for them at the mall, but she still had yet to find the perfect gift for her mom, who had helped her through so much and who was always there with a listening ear and a word of encouragement and support.

After Janie spent twenty minutes searching for a parking place, she finally found one—about a mile from the store. On her way in, she noticed an elderly lady struggling to make her way to the door. It appeared to Janie that the woman had needed to park far away from the entrance just like Janie had, but it was a much greater hardship on this lady who was struggling to walk so far unaided.

Janie's attention was immediately arrested by this sweet-looking old woman and her heart went out to her.

"Excuse me—Ma'am?" Janie said as she approached the dear lady who had already captured her heart. "Ma'am?" Janie repeated a little louder as the lady didn't appear to hear the first time.

"Wh-what? Oh—yes, Dear. Oh, my. You gave me a bit of a fright.

May I help you?" The sweet lady asked with a smile so bright that her blue eyes sparkled and shined.

"Well, Ma'am, I was wondering if you would allow me to offer you my arm as we walk into the store." Janie suggested with a smile.

"Oh—Dear, now you don't have to do that. I'm sure you are in a terrible hurry—people always are these days. And Christmas time—a time meant for slowing down and reflecting on our Savior's birth— seems to be one of those times when people are even busier than usual," the sweet lady finished.

"Please," Janie said sincerely, as she again offered her arm to the sweetheart. "I want to."

"Well, thank you, Dear. This is so kind of you. My name is Alice. May I ask the name of the lady kind enough to take notice of an old lady like me?" Alice asked with a twinkle in her eye.

"My name is Janie, Miss Alice. And it is my pleasure to help," Janie said from her heart as they made their way slowly to the storefront in the busy parking lot. Janie walked on the outside to protect Miss Alice from cars, and she was on the alert to steer her clear of danger.

"Tell me, Dear—what made you stop for me?" Miss Alice asked as she looked up at Janie's face from her position of being hunched over Janie's arm.

"Well, Miss Alice," Janie began, feeling a need to share her heart, "My own Grandma passed away two years ago in December. I have no family of my own, and my Grandma always took special care of me. I miss her terribly, but whenever I see a dear lady like you with silver hair, it softens my heart and gives me one more opportunity to show love to someone like my Grandma—someone who may need my help. It makes me feel closer to her and nearer to the ache all at the same time. But it never fails to leave a warm glow in its wake. Miss Alice, the truth is that you are doing much more for my heart right now than I can ever do for you," Janie confessed.

Miss Alice stopped and looked up again at Janie with a discerning look. "Hmmm," she said to herself and then began walking again—more slowly now.

"Janie," Miss Alice said, "I hope you don't mind my asking this, but would you say that you are a lonely person?" And again Miss Alice looked up at Janie with that discerning look in her crystal clear blue eyes.

"Well…" Janie kind of faltered here and looked down. She didn't admit to many people that she felt alone. In fact, there was only one person in the world she had ever told: her mom.

"It's okay, Dear. You don't have to answer that. Let me just tell you that you have been such a blessing to me today by noticing me and by stopping to offer me your assistance. I lost my husband a few years back and I had to move into an assisted living center down the road from here—do you know the one?"

At Janie's nod, Miss Alice continued, "Well, Jesus has been my Best Friend through this time, and through reading and obeying His Word, the Bible, I have come to know the truth that when I reach out and love others, I forget myself. I experience much joy and warmth in my heart as I reach out to my fellow residents, many of whom are lonely like me." Miss Alice paused as they neared the storefront.

When they reached the front of the store, they stopped and Miss Alice smiled. "My Dear, I would like to invite you to our Christmas party at the Assisted Living Center on Christmas Eve. It will be at 5 pm and won't go very late. There will be food and fun, and you would have many people like me to show your love to. In the New Year, I invite you to come again to visit as often as you can. Your presence would be very welcome for so many of us who never have visitors." Miss Alice said to Janie with a smile.

"Why, I don't know…" Janie said in uncertainty.

She was taken completely by surprise by an idea that had never occurred to her. "I will have to think about it and see what I can do… but that does sound like a lovely idea," Janie admitted. "Let me walk you over here where we can get you a cart to hang on to," Janie suggested.

"Oh, thank you, Dear!" Miss Alice said as they headed that way.

Once she had her cart, Miss Alice looked up one last time and said, "Thank you, Dear. Thank you for blessing my heart this Christmas and for sharing with me a little bit of yours. Always know that

God made you to be a blessing. God bless you, Dear, with a very Merry Christmas!"

"Thank you, Miss Alice! Merry Christmas!" Janie said, truly meaning it for the first time that season.

As Janie took a hand basket for herself and went to look for the perfect gift for her mom, she realized something—God had just reached down and given her a very special Christmas gift. He had given her the gift of love in the form of Miss Alice. He had softened her own heart and allowed her to show love to someone else— and now she had this sense of joy and peace and warmth inside that hadn't been there before, which was pointing her gaze back to her Lord and Savior, Jesus Christ, who had been born so that she may have life forever in Him. The thought struck Janie—Maybe all that I need to be whole and complete truly CAN be found in Jesus.

Janie smiled and found the perfect gift for her mom—a battery-powered back massager with extra batteries and peppermint foot lotion with several pair of cute cozy socks. Her mom would love these—and she deserved to be pampered!

Janie also picked out a nice little gift to bring to the Christmas Eve party at the Assisted Living Center. It was a small nativity piece—a perfect reminder of the reason we celebrate Christmas.

Janie had found a place to give love—something that had been missing in her life. She would go there and be surrounded by those who needed her at Miss Alice's home in the Assisted Living

Center—but Janie knew that she would be the one to be blessed most of all!

As Janie drove home that evening through all of the crazy traffic, there was peace inside of her as she prayed a prayer of thanksgiving to her Heavenly Father, who loved her too much to leave her alone on Christmas. She knew now that God was always with her—and she knew now that she was Never Alone.

Day 4:

Rescued by Love

When someone comes into your life, you don't always know if that someone is going to change everything. That happened to me five years ago when a big black dog named Max appeared on my doorstep.

Little did I know that things would never be the same for me again.

But let me back up and introduce myself…

My name is Sarah—Sarah Raine. Five years ago, I lived a structured and very orderly lifestyle. I was always on time for every appointment, climbing the corporate ladder, and making a name for myself in this world. I was single, busy, married to my work, and loving every minute of it…or so I thought. Then I met Max.

For all of my adult life, I never thought I really needed anyone in my life. I thought I was self- sufficient—the best this world had to offer. Max taught me otherwise.

You see, Max just showed up at my doorstep one night. He was just waiting there, looking for all the world like he had been waiting the whole day just to see me. He calmly sat and looked up at me with soulful eyes and a lopsided doggy grin.

Honestly, it kind of freaked me out. I mean, where had he come from? Was he confused? Why was he at my house?

Max was a very large black dog with a white blaze on his chest, and to see him just sitting on my doorstep was somewhat intimidating to my short 5 foot 3 inch self—but I finally got up the courage and shooed him away. After all, there was no way that I was going to feed someone else's dog.

When I shooed him off with my briefcase, Max just looked at me as though he pitied me, gave me another doggy grin, and plodded off to who knows where—I assumed to find a meal.

The next night I came home late again from work, and who did I find waiting for me but the same big black dog with the lopsided grin. Again I shooed him away, thinking, *This dog is really* **confused!** *What on earth is the matter with him?* And again, Max just looked at me as though he pitied me, gave me that huge doggy grin, and went on his way.

Well, night after night, during my company's busiest season— when I was working seven days a week, driven by greed, pride, and a lust for power, I would come home and find this dog on my doorstep just waiting calmly for me with those big soulful eyes and a big tongue hanging out of the side of his mouth. And every day, I would shoo him away—but I'm telling you, I began to look forward to coming home to this ever faithful dog that never missed a day of greeting me.

One night I came home and Max was not waiting for me. I had no idea how attached I had become to him until he was not there. I found myself feeling like something was missing, and I knew it had to do with Max—as I had secretly named him.

I had never fed Max or even given him water, and yet every day for a whole month—without fail—he was there on my doorstep to welcome me home during the busiest time of the year for me when I made time for nothing or no one else but my work.

I never saw Max again after that night, and I never found out what happened to him. But do you know what I think?

I think that God sent Max to my doorstep to send me a wake-up call and to remind me of something that I was missing that I hadn't experienced, nurtured, or sought out since I was a child.

That something was Unconditional Love.

Yes, Max was just a dog, but God used him as a way to show me what it is like to experience love from someone who never received anything good in return from me.

After the night that Max did not return, I did some very real soul-searching. I needed to know the reason that I was so sad over the loss of an animal that I had not even wanted in my life in the first place. As I sought to understand what had caused this sudden void I felt inside, I realized something. Max's tireless devotion reminded me of God and His love.

I had learned about God in church many years ago as a child, but I had not thought of God seriously since I was very young. When I was young, I believed in Jesus Christ and received Him into my life as my Savior to forgive me from my sins. Since then, I had grown up and away from God, His Word, His people in the church, and His love. It had come to the point where none of them had any place in my life.

But God had loved me all those years that I had been away from Him, chasing after worldly success, and He had received NOTHING good from me in return— just like Max. Max had waited faithfully for me every day while never receiving even one kind word or a pat on the head.

The night that I came home late from work and did not see Max waiting for me was December 24th five years ago—the night before Christmas—Christmas Eve.

You see, I was in marketing at the time for a toy company whose sales were sky-rocketing. They had all of the year's hottest toys that Christmas season, and I was working late every day up until Christmas Eve promoting sales—completely married to my work with no family to speak of at all.

But something changed that Christmas. God rescued me from a life that was full of worldly success but was completely empty of purpose and meaning. God rescued me through the love of a stray K-9 named Max. Max's unconditional love pointed me back to the perfect love of God and of His Son, Jesus Christ. I will never forget that Christmas.

That New Year started a whole new life for me.

Today, five years later, my life looks completely different. I am still not married to anyone—God has not brought that man into my life—but neither am I married to my work. I recommitted my life to Jesus Christ and surrendered my life to doing what He desires me to do.

Today, I belong to a church where I help out with the children's ministry. The children and their families take turns coming to my house where they do crafts, bake, talk, share, experience God's love, and play with my two rescue dogs, Shannon and Jay.

My life is finally full of God's love, and God is so very good...

You know, the truth is that for my entire life, God was always good—I just had not taken the time to slow down and notice it for years.

This is my story.

I am Sarah Raine, and I have been Rescued by Love.

Day 5:

A Reason
To Rejoice at Christmas

Frost-covered pine boughs,

Snow-covered banks.

Palm trees with Christmas

lights, And soldiers in tanks.

Do these things go together?

In small, maybe not.

But when you look at the big picture,

Christmas can be cold or it can be hot.

Look at the whole world—

We all experience Christmas differently.

Some may be at war

While others are at peace.

So wherever this Christmas finds you,

May one thing still be true.

May Jesus be the One you love,

For He came to earth for you!

Day 6:

Christmas Delights

Snow-covered blossoms

And pretty twinkling lights.

Snowmen dressed in scarves and prancing reindeer—

What wonderful sights!

Stories by the fire

And hot cocoa, too!

Twelve days of Christmas

And Grandma's thick, filling stew!

A bright red cardinal

Ready to fly,

Snowflakes falling down

From a star-studded sky.

As we say good night,

We remember the One

Who has blessed us so much

By giving us His Son.

For all these Christmas Delights

Could never top the love

That God showed each one of us

By sending His Son, Jesus, from above.

Day 7:

Christmas is About Jesus

Army Green

Brick Red

Snow White

Icicle Lights

Hanging from above.

Dreams of home

Far Away

And yet I wonder why?

So much suffering—

So much hate.

Could it be because…

Sin exists

In this world

Inside of you and me?

It is ugly

And it is dark—

But up ahead—

Do you see?

A Light so Bright

Shining up

For all the world

To see!

It is the Light of God's Love—

Oh can you feel its warmth?

Beautiful, shining down on all—

No matter our figure or form.

My friend, in this season Of Christmas cheer,

May we truly know the One Who came near

That we could be with Him forever,

Knowing that to His heart, we are very dear.

For Christmas is about Jesus,

As is every day of the year.

Walking with Him in every season,

Through every joy and every tear.

Yes, Christmas is about Jesus—

May we never miss His call—

For He is worthy of our Love—

Our life, our surrender, our ALL!

Day 8:

Sweet Dreams of Christmas

Christmas is a beautiful

Time of the year.

There's something special in the air,

And so much to hold dear.

Red and white,

Green and Gold,

Heart-warming songs,

And tales of old—

So much fun

To be had.

Cookies with Mom

And projects with Dad.

Presents wrapped

Under the tree

Love to pass

Between you and me.

Frost is on

The window pane.

Hot Cocoa in your mug

With a cheery candy cane.

And last but not least,

A Nativity scene

Complete with mother and child

How sweetly she leans!

Snowflakes are falling

And softly covering the wintry scape

You cozy up to the fire with a book—

The heat feels so great!

Your book is getting good,

But then you nod off to sleep.

Sweet dreams, my friend!

May all your dreams be sweet!

Day 9:

What Are You Getting For Christmas?

What are you getting for Christmas?

Do you have big plans?

Will you see a big parade

Or a marching band?

Are you going on a trip

To visit family?

Or are you staying right at home

Around your Christmas tree?

Either way,

I know one thing to be true:

Only if Jesus is number One,

Will all be right with you.

He can give you peace

No matter the season of life.

He will be your joy.

He can show you how to avoid strife.

What do I want for Christmas?

To have peace inside my heart.

Right now and always—

Never to depart.

Lord, I love You,

And I need

To have You near

Always to me.

Thank You, Lord,

That You will never ever leave!

In Jesus' Name,

Amen!

Day 10:

Miss Martha

I remember a time when life was all about being the best that I could be. It was just about working hard, being as good as I could be, and making a name for myself in the world. That all changed the year I met Miss Martha.

I was home from college for the summer that year, and I had decided to volunteer for some community service, helping the elderly. I ended up being assigned to help Mrs. Martha Culbert at her home. I did her yardwork, some painting, and a few little maintenance tasks that a husband would usually do.

Miss Martha, as she preferred to be called, had lost her husband a couple of years back, and she was getting to the point to where those tasks were more than she could handle alone.

Miss Martha and I hit it off from the beginning.

She insisted on calling me by my given name,

"Nathaniel," instead of by "Nat," which is what everyone else called me. On the first day, I tended to her lawn and flower beds. After I was finished mowing the lawn, I remember that she brought a tall glass of refreshing lemonade out to me. While we stood in the shade of her oak tree, I took a break, and she began talking to me.

"Isn't this yard such a blessing, Nathaniel? I praise God every day for this healthy, green grass; these beautiful flowers; my big, strong oak tree; and for the way He makes them grow so that I can enjoy them.

They provide for an entire ecosystem in my backyard: worms, insects, lizards, birds, squirrels. They all live here with me, and God supports each of us. As He says in His Word in Psalm 104, "O Lord, how manifold are Your works! In wisdom You have made them all. The earth is full of Your possessions…These all wait for you, that You may give them their food in due season. What You give them they gather in; You open Your hand, they are filled with good. You hide Your face, they are troubled; You take away their breath, they die and return to their dust. You send forth Your Spirit, they are created; and You renew the face of the earth" (Psalm 104:24; 27-30).

Miss Martha's talk of God took me by surprise. In fact, it was like a bucket of cold water being tossed in my face. You see, God was not a popular theme on my college campus, to say the least. In fact, the subject of God was avoided like the plague. But after I got over my initial shock, I heard something interesting that I decided to ask her about.

"Miss Martha, you say that comes from God's Word… as in, the Bible? I never knew anything like that was in the Bible."

"It's a wonderful passage, isn't it?" she asked. At my smile—at this point I figured that was the safest response—she continued, "My beautiful backyard

ecosystem reminds me of another portion of God's Word. In Matthew 6, Jesus says, '"Look at the birds of the air, for they neither sow nor reap nor gather into barns; yet your heavenly Father feeds them. Are you not of more value than they? Which of you by worrying can add one cubit to his stature? So why do you worry about clothing? Consider the lilies of the field, how they grow: they neither toil nor spin; and yet I say to you that even Solomon in all his glory was not arrayed like one of these. Now if God so clothes the grass of the field, which today is, and tomorrow is thrown into the oven, will He not much more clothe you, O you of little faith?

Therefore do not worry, saying 'What shall we eat?' or 'What shall we drink?' or 'What shall we wear?' For after all these things the Gentiles seek. For your heavenly Father knows that you need all these things. But seek first the kingdom of God and His righteousness, and all these things shall be added to you. Therefore, do not worry about tomorrow, for tomorrow will worry about its own things. Sufficient for the day is its own trouble'" (Matthew 6:26-34). I learned this truth of not worrying and seeking God first the hard way. I can tell you about it sometime, if you like," Miss Martha finished.

"I think I'd like to hear about that, thank you," I said. My interest surprised me, since college life had caused me to become very skeptical of all things related to God. But, in spite of myself, something deep inside of me was responding to the strength of this woman's convictions and her obvious, deep love for her God. It caused me to come face-to-face with something I had never seen before, and—quite frankly—I was curious.

As I finished weeding the flowerbeds and saw all of the different forms of life up close, I could not help but think back on what Miss Martha had said and the passages she had quoted. They seemed to come alive as I wondered, "Is there really a God somewhere that provides for these creatures, or is it just nature—does it just happen by itself? Is there really a greater Someone who cares about me who I can trust to take care of all of my needs… Someone I was made to serve?"

These thoughts were deep. I considered them for a little while, but as soon as I left Miss Martha's house that day, they promptly left my mind. God was not finished with me yet, however. As I would come to know later, Miss Martha was praying for me and for the seeds that God had planted in my heart that day in the form of the words she spoke. She prayed that my heart would be open to receiving His Word, and that my life would be transformed from the inside out by His love. This dear woman prayed in faith, believing that God's will would be accomplished in my life and trusted the outcome to Him.

Later on that week, I went back to Miss Martha's house to do some painting in one of her bathrooms.

"Welcome back, Nathaniel! It's so good to see you!" Miss Martha greeted me.

I wondered inwardly if this woman was always so cheerful. Miss Martha showed me back to the bathroom that I would be painting, and before long, I had started the job and was whistling a happy tune. It did not take long for Miss Martha to join me.

"Do you mind if I keep you company?" she asked me from the doorway.

"Not at all," I said.

"Isn't indoor plumbing such a blessing?" Miss Martha commented pleasantly.

I smiled her way. I honestly had never really thought about it before.

"My mother lived in a house that had no indoor plumbing when she was a girl. She taught us to give thanks to God for something that seemed so commonplace to us. She also taught us a greater lesson about thankfulness. It comes from the Bible. 1 Thessalonians 5:16-18 says, 'Rejoice always, pray without ceasing, in everything give thanks; for this is the will of God in Christ Jesus for you.' She taught us that no matter what is going on in our lives, there is always a reason to rejoice, for we have everlasting life in Jesus Christ and love from the Heavenly Father.

Whether trouble arises or good times come, we should always

rejoice and be in prayer, talking to our Lord, giving anxious thoughts over to Him, pleading for assistance, or praising His Name. On top of all of this, we are to give thanks to God in everything, and we can know that when we do all of these things, we are in the center of His will for us, for it says so in His Word. Oh, God is so wonderful, isn't He?" Miss Martha said with shining eyes.

Again, I simply turned and smiled, then continued painting. What could I say? I had never thought of any of this before. I had no intelligent thoughts on the subject.

"Well, I'll go and fix you a snack, so you can take a break," she said as she disappeared into the kitchen.

As I listened to noises coming from the other room, I thought about what she had said. This God thing was the way she lived her life, and it was affecting me. What did I think about it? Right now, I honestly did not know, but I did want to hear more. The thought occurred to me that, though I was away from school, I still seemed to be getting an education… one that my college did not offer.

When Miss Martha came back, announcing that the snack was ready, I happily followed her to her kitchen nook table where a place had been set for me. I was eager to spend more time with this delightful lady.

"You know, Nathaniel," Miss Martha said as I began eating, "though I was taught the Word of God from a very young age, I only went through the motions of Christianity for many years of my life. I had not surrendered my life to truly serve God or seek Him and obey Him first above all else. I went back and forth from trying to be good in my own power to being just downright self-absorbed and intent on making myself happy."

"But what's wrong with trying to be good?" I asked. I could see how being self-absorbed could be bad, but I thought that being good was what I was supposed to do. I thought it was the right way to live.

"Jesus said that there is only One who is good, and that is God (Luke 18:19)," Miss Martha answered. "I didn't have the ability to be good by myself, and that's why I kept failing. I didn't have the Spirit of God inside of me to produce the fruit of the Spirit, which is 'love, joy, peace, patience, kindness, goodness, faithfulness, gentleness, and self-control' (Galatians 5:22-23).

"I eventually fell into a deep depression. I was incapacitated for some time. I dropped out of the college I had been taking classes at, and I quit my part time job. I lived off of my college savings for a while. Life seemed so dark. I just wanted to sleep all of the time or lose myself in vain activities that took no brain power and brought passing pleasure. I ate large quantities of sweets and read a lot of penny novels, society magazines, and newspaper columns. I tried to get lost in the lives of others, living through their highs and lows, while I withdrew further from the world around me and deeper into myself.

"But all throughout that time, those verses from the Bible that I had learned when I was young stayed in the recesses of my mind, keeping me from giving up entirely. Though I felt so weighted down, like I was in a black hole with no escape, there always remained a distant ray of hope. My life was not over.

"I knew what I had to do, but I just could not bring myself to do it, until finally, one day, I was ready. I had enough of the darkness! I wanted out, and I knew the Way. I got out my Bible in my room, opened the blinds to the window by my bed, and I started crying out to God. I poured out my heart to Him. And as I did, His Holy Spirit led me from verse to verse in the Bible that I had learned from my childhood that I thought I had forgotten.

"God is so good! He brought me through that time. He taught me that the only way to eternal life is through faith in His Son, Jesus Christ. It is a free gift from Him that I can never earn. The Bible says in 1 John 5, 'whatever is born of God overcomes the world. And this is the victory that has overcome the world—our faith. Who is he who overcomes the world, but he who believes that Jesus is the Son of God?' (1 John 5:4-5) Oh, Nathaniel, God has been so very good to this old woman and blessed her with such a beautiful life in Him," Miss Martha finished with tears of thankfulness and deep emotion in her voice.

"I think I would have to agree that you live a beautiful life, Miss Martha. But what do you mean by 'overcoming the world'?" I asked.

"Oh, I'm sorry, dear. The 'world' here means all of the sin, death, and evil temptations that are in the world that entered into it in the beginning when Adam first sinned against God," Miss Martha responded.

"You mean Adam and Eve from the Bible? You believe that story is true?" I asked. I was amazed at what I was hearing.

"Oh, yes. Very much so. Jesus would never have had to die if that story was not true," Miss Martha said with deep conviction.

"You've given me a lot to think about. Thank you for sharing your story with me. I better get back to painting your bathroom, so it gets done today," I said as I got up from the table.

"Oh, yes, of course! You go right ahead, dear.

Thank you," Miss Martha responded as she ushered me from the kitchen.

As I went back to the painting, I stayed deep in thought. "Wow, she hasn't always been this cheerful. Her life is dramatically different today from what it used to be. Can I ignore that kind of power? Do I want to?"

When I left Miss Martha's that evening, I found myself wanting to read from this Book that simply defined the incredible woman that I was getting to know. Since I did not own a Bible, I drove to the nearest bookstore on my way home and bought an inexpensive one.

"This should be interesting," I thought to myself. I never would have dreamed that I would be buying and reading a Bible over my summer holiday.

Over the next couple of weeks, I visited Miss Martha three more times, helping her to change light bulbs in hard-to-reach places and fixing odds and ends here and there in her house. Every time that I went to help her, I went away realizing that she had given me another precious piece of herself and a greater understanding of her faith. She told me about a magazine that she subscribed to that answered a lot of the questions that I was asking. She gave me several of her old copies to keep.

I wish I could say that my life was magically transformed after those few weeks. But the truth is, I am very thankful that it did not happen that way.

On my last summer day with Miss Martha, when I was telling her goodbye, she said to me, "Nathaniel, God loves you. He sent His Son into a world that hated Him, so that He could die for your sins, because He wanted you to know Him. Seek Him out. Seek Him with all of your heart, and you will find Him. God has promised this to be true in His Word (Matthew 7:7-8; Luke 11:9-13; Hebrews 11:6). Believe in Him, and He will never let you down. God bless you. And always remember that I am praying for you." She then gave me a quick hug and sent me on my way.

The rest of my summer was full of activities, but I did find time to read the magazines that she had given me. When I went back to school, I continued to read the Bible that I had bought, and I started going to a local church that taught from the Bible. I attended church every Sunday morning and listened to what the pastor had to say. I did as Miss Martha had advised and found a church that believed that the Bible is the unquestionable Word of God and that it is absolutely true. I eventually developed friendships with some people who attended there. They loved God, and they lived their lives to obey Him.

That fall, I came to know Jesus as my own personal Lord and Savior. I learned to rejoice as Miss Martha had spoken of. I walked side by side with a man who had been living faithfully for the Lord for many years. He took me under his wing and taught me a lot about living the Word of God by the power of the Holy Spirit. He taught me in practical ways, and he made himself available to me. He called it discipleship.

I began to learn to pray without ceasing and to give thanks in all circumstances. The peace that filled me when I gave my cares to Christ and put my trust in Him—being full of thankfulness regardless of how I was feeling—was beyond anything that I had ever known.

When I went home for Christmas that year, it was with an overflowing heart. I was full of the wonder of God's love, and it was a Christmas like no other.

While I was home, I stopped to spend time with Miss Martha. I brought her a single, long-stemmed red rose when I went to see her.

"Miss Martha, your prayers were answered," I said as I stood on her doorstep with a huge smile on my face. I held the rose out to her, "This is for you, Miss Martha, for giving me the most precious gift that one person can give another. You gave me the gift of Christ's love. Now I know Him, too. May God bless you always." I stepped into her loving arms as we cried together, with hearts full of thankfulness for what the Lord had done in our lives.

It has been many years since that day. Miss Martha has since gone on to be with our Lord, and I have experienced many highs and lows in my own walk with God. But He has never left me and has never forsaken me. As Miss Martha said so many years ago, "He has never let me down." For His gift of love to me, I always find a reason to rejoice.

Every summer, I take a trip back to my hometown and visit Miss Martha's grave. I always bring a single, long-stemmed red rose, and I remember. I remember the gift that she gave me so long ago, and I ask my Lord to use me like He used His beautiful servant, Miss Martha. For, where would I be if she had not been willing to share the Truth of God's Love with me?

Day 11:

Dreams by the Fireplace

A little girl sat up by the fire, staring into its flames. She was thankful for its warmth on such a coldand frosty night.

The rest of the town was preparing for Christmas, but in the Miller household, Christmas was a thing existing only in dreams. That did not keep Rebecca from dreaming, though.

Rebecca had a beautiful heart and a healthy imagination. Together with the two, she dreamed many dreams by firelight of warm, cozy, fur-lined coats and spicy gingerbread. She dreamed of shiny, brand-new toys for her little brother and beautiful satin gowns for her mother and older sister, complete with white kid gloves.

Becca saved her dreaming for the nights, because there was no time for her dreams during the day—there was always work to be done.

But at night, things were different. Mother allowed Becca to stay up by the fire for as long as she desired. It was the one gift Mother thought she could offer to her dear daughter who worked so hard inside the home at such a tender age. Becca's mother knew that her daughter was a dreamer and that she used such times when she was alone to think and dream.

Mrs. Miller wanted to encourage her daughter's dreams, so she gave her this special time each night, especially during the winter when the days were so short.

Tonight as Becca lay on a blanket before the fire, gazing into its flames, she began to dream of what it must be like to buy candy and oranges and ingredients for Christmas baking.

What must it be like to go shopping for Christmas gifts--to have a Christmas tree with glowing lights?

Rebecca's father had died when her mother was pregnant with her younger brother, Jack, and before that, he had been very ill. Becca could not remember a time when her mother and older sister were not working outside the home to support them. Because of this, Becca had taken on the household responsibilities at a young age.

Life was not easy, and the Miller family only had enough income to just barely pay the bills and put food on the table. Rebecca was starting to lose heart at age 10, and this is where our story begins— for it was this year at Christmas time that everything changed for young Rebecca and her family.

On a day when Rebecca had been doing some extra cleaning inside their home, she uncovered a treasure that she had never before known existed. The treasure was an old family Bible. It had been handed down through the generations on her dad's side, but her mother had tucked it away after Mr. Miller's death.

Instead of seeking comfort in its pages, Mrs. Miller had found the Bible a painful reminder of the man she had loved so dearly who had been taken from her all too soon.

When Rebecca discovered it, she truly felt that she had found a treasure, for not only had she discovered a link to her father and her family heritage, but she had also received a new book to read—a BIG one!

Now, Rebecca could not ever remember being taught about God, the Bible, or Jesus, but she LOVED to read, and there was never any extra money for new books. So, without asking, Rebecca carefully took the old Bible out of hiding with the purpose of reading it every night as she stayed up by the fire.

What Rebecca found in that Bible ended up changing her life. She was a voracious reader, but what she read in this newly discovered Book produced more questions in her young heart than she had ever known before.

Because she thought it was just another book, she started at the beginning, fully intending to read it straight through to the end. But it was unlike any other book she had ever read.

After three nights of reading, she went to her mother and mentioned the Book to her. She had so many questions, and they were begging to be answered.

When she asked her mother about the Book during dinner preparations, she watched as a pained look crossed her mother's face.

Mrs. Miller said, "Rebecca, the Bible is God's Book. It is His Word to us. In it, we learn of our need for Him and of the Hope we have because He sent His Son, Jesus."

"Who is Jesus?" Rebecca asked her mother.

"He is the reason for Christmas, dear. Christmas is the celebration of His birth. I'm so sorry that I have not taught you about God. It is good that you are asking these questions," Rebecca's mother said as she stepped away from the dinner preparations and pulled out a chair.

"Come here, Rebecca... I have a story to tell you.

When your Father died, I was angry at God. I blamed Him for taking my husband—your father—away from us. How could a loving God do something like that to our family? We had always loved God and served Him so faithfully. But I was wrong to blame God. God has proved to be faithful even when I have not been. He has provided for us—not always in the ways that I had hoped—but all of our needs have been met. I am beginning to see that this life is not about being comfortable here on earth. It should be about following Jesus and sharing in His sufferings, that we may one day join Him in eternity, just as your Father has," Mrs. Miller said with a far-off look in her eye and tears rolling down her cheek.

"But who is Jesus, Mother?" Rebecca asked again.

"My dear Rebecca, I am going to introduce you to Him. Through Him, you will have the opportunity to meet God as your Heavenly Father," Mrs. Miller said. "I will begin reading with you, your sister, and your brother in the evenings from the Gospels of Matthew, Mark, Luke, and John. In these books of the Bible, you will meet Jesus, and I will tell you how you can come to know Him in a relationship between you and Him."

"I'm still confused, Mother," Rebecca said, "But I want to know more. Are you sure we will have time for this?"

"Let me worry about the work this time, dear Rebecca. This is so very important, and it is my fault that it has been neglected for so very long. We will

begin tonight," Mrs. Miller said with a warm smile to her sweet daughter as she stood and they once again resumed their dinner preparations.

That night, Mrs. Miller opened the old Family Bible before the fire and began to read to her three children from the Gospel of Matthew. She answered all of their questions, for her husband had taught her well.

As she taught them, she prayed in her heart to God and listened to the One whom she had distanced herself from so long ago. She came to Him, confessing her wrongdoing in not sharing the Truth with her children and for running from the Truth for so many years. She knew that God forgave her, for He truly is faithful even when we are not (2 Timothy 2:13; 1 John 1:9).

Things began to change for the Miller family that night. They began to pray together, and that Christmas, Rebeca met Jesus and began following Him as her Savior and Lord.

Hope had entered their world and changed everything. Though their circumstances did not change, joy had entered into their hearts. They had each begun to place their trust in the goodness of God—whether they could see good things happening now or not. Each of them had been learning to live for a future good to be revealed one day when God's glory is revealed to all.

Their joy had begun to flow not from the present but from a future hope of being face to face with Jesus—the One who had died and risen again that they may have life and wholeness with Him forever. Life may never be easy for them in the present—but they had a joyous future to look forward to. Any present and earthly comforts that God chose to give them in this world would simply be icing on the cake—but never the main attraction in their relationship with God. This family had learned that earthly blessings would come and go, but God and His precious promises are forever.

Rebecca was no longer spending her nights by the fire, dreaming of finer things. Instead, she would fall asleep by the fire, praying and talking to her Lord— thanking Him for all of her blessings— especially for Jesus. She talked to Him about her needs and her deepest desires, and she always praised Him for how great and AWESOME and GOOD He is.

Yes, Rebecca's life had changed, and it had all started the day she found a dusty old Book when she was being faithful in the duties assigned to her at home. God had seen this young girl's plight and He had made a way for her to know Him. God had remembered her mother—He had seen her crushed spirit—and He had revived it.

God had brought hope to the entire family—a hope that would only grow as the days passed and their trust in God deepened.

Yes, Rebecca now knew God through His Son, Jesus Christ, and she knew that God was, in fact, ALWAYS very good and she could ALWAYS trust Him with all of her heart.

That Christmas, Rebecca's family still did not have a Christmas tree, but Rebecca had Jesus in her heart, and she knew she had great reason to celebrate— both now at Christmas time and forevermore!

Day 12:

Fireplace Dreams

A Cozy fireplace

Is the perfect place to dream,

With a cup of cocoa in your hand,

Letting off swirls of steam.

You dream of days gone by,

You dream of days to come.

You dream of Christmas up ahead—

All the laughter and the fun.

You dream of fuzzy Santa hats—

You dream of big red bows.

You dream of serene nativity scenes

And a reindeer's bright red nose.

All these dreams of yours

Bring to your face a smile.

They bring warmth to your heart

That will last for a while.

But as you sip your cocoa,

Your mind turns to one more thing

While the bell-chimes on your clock

Begin their nightly ring.

You have forgotten

The most important part:

The reason for Christmas—

The season's very heart.

So you begin to pray—

Instead of dream—

By the fireside

As peace comes like a gentle stream.

Your heart turns back now

To warm thoughts of Christmas

And the Savior who came to save you:

His name is Jesus.

Day 13:

The Best Christmas Gift

Sometimes I think we get intoxicated with the nostalgia and warm fuzzy feelings we associate with Christmas.

We can depend on these nostalgic feelings so much that when they are missing, we feel deep sadness and loss for a bygone time when all felt right, beautiful, lovely, and bright.

The problem with this?

We miss the point of Christmas—or the very point of life, for that matter.

Warm, fuzzy feelings are lovely—they make us feel comfy and cozy, but are they reality or just an illusion?

…Or maybe they are a taste of something better to come.

The Bible says that every good and perfect gift is from above (James 1:17). That does not include treasures where moth and rust destroy or where thieves break in and steal (Matthew 6:19).

I need this reminder very much.

The truth is that it is so easy to focus on all that this world has to offer. It is here. It is now. And all of it is staring right at us—daring us to taste, to feel, and to touch.

The problem?

Enough is never enough. The things of this world will never satisfy the deep cravings of our souls.

The result?

A deep emptiness within. The solution?

Jesus.

We must put Jesus first.

When we do, does that mean we will get all those warm fuzzies back?

Maybe—but maybe not. The feelings are not our prize—and they are not to be relied upon (Jeremiah 17:9). Feelings can lead us astray.

So what is the perfect gift? Jesus.

Jesus is the treasure that can never be stolen from us. We have every spiritual blessing in Him, and every promise of God's is ours in Him (2 Peter 1:3; 2 Corinthians 1:20).

But it is Jesus Himself who is our Love. He is the One who should be our Delight.

Every day, we should awake with Him on our minds, spend every waking moment rejoicing in His presence, and go to sleep with Him filling our thoughts.

This is how He wants us to live.

He wants to consume our lives and produce great fruit in us.

Jesus is our perfect gift.

Every day, He is our Life-giving present from God the Heavenly Father.

Warm, fuzzy feelings are great when they come, but they are so very fleeting and unreliable.

Jesus is the opposite.

He is the same yesterday, today, and forever (Hebrews 13:8).

He will never change, and He will never forsake His own (Hebrews 13:5).

Are you fully experiencing God's greatest gift? Am I?

I pray that this year, we will spend every day— not chasing elusive feelings that are here one day and gone the next—but instead, placing all of our hope in the grace to be brought to us at the revelation of Jesus Christ our Lord (1 Peter 1:13).

We have a **living** hope, and it is ours in Jesus (1 Peter 1:3).

If we suffer in this life, may it be for doing good—may we give glory to God even as we suffer, for those who suffer for the name of Jesus are blessed (1 Peter 4:12-19).

Remember that suffering will not last forever. God has promised to use it—along with all things—to make His children who belong to Him more like Jesus (1 Peter 5:10; Romans 8:28-29).

So this Christmas, as we sit by a cozy fire, may we talk to and enjoy the presence of our precious Lord Jesus.

May Jesus be our everything, and may He be the One we walk and talk with at every hour of the day.

May our lives be lived to serve Him and willingly suffer for His name if He asks us to.

May we not only recognize our need for Jesus, but may our **desire** for Him blaze stronger than our cozy living room fire.

God bless you, Friend, and Merry Christmas!

May Jesus be the best gift you enjoy this season and every day of the year!

In Jesus' Name, Amen!

Day 14:

The Christmas Stars

Rosie looked up into the night sky and gazed inwonder at the stars.

"Lord, there are so many! And to think, You know how many there are, for You created them and You know all things."

Rosie continued her walk in silence for a time. This was her time of the day for quiet and reflection with her Lord. The nights were getting brisk now, fall having just begun in her small Illinois town.

Rosie was a first-year teacher and tonight she was thinking of what small thing she could do for her young students for Christmas. It would have to be something small. After all, she had very little money. But she wanted it to be meaningful, for each one of her school children had a special place in her heart reserved just for them.

She thought of Sally, who had drawn a daisy dancing in the sun and given it to her teacher, saying, "Miss Rosie, this daisy is me and it's dancing because it's happy to be under the sun, just like I'm happy to be in your class." Rosie remembered the warm glow that had filled her heart that day as she smiled at Sally and thanked her for such a beautiful treasure. For to her, it was one.

Then there was Mikey, the smallest boy of the class who was a joy to everyone. He may have been the smallest, but he had the largest heart of them all. He saw the best in everyone, and his words were like sweet honey that coated the heart. Rosie loved to see him interact with the other children, for his very presence softened them and made them appreciate love in its purest form.

And she could never forget Gertrude. She went by Gerty now and loved her teacher, but at the beginning of the year, she had been quite the challenge. She bullied other kids and stole their lunches. During class time, she spoke back to Rosie with defiance in her voice and a refusal to submit to her authority. Rosie had been at her wits' end to know what to do. One day, when Gertrude pushed Mikey to the ground outside during recess causing him to cry, Rosie had come running from inside the schoolhouse. "What happened here?" She had asked. Mikey stayed on the ground, silently sniffing, and Marie didn't get any answers right away.

Later that day, after Gertrude had been punished and the children had been dismissed, Mikey came up to his teacher, Miss Rosie.

"Miss Rosie?"

"Why yes, Mikey? What can I do for you?" Rosie had asked.

"Well, ya know when I was cryin' earlier?"

"Yes, I do. Gertrude was very wrong to push you down like that," Rosie had said.

"Well, that's just it. I wasn't cryin' 'cause she pushed me. I was cryin' 'cause of what she said."

"Oh." This surprised Rosie. "What did she say?" she had asked.

"Well, she was mad at me 'cause I was bein' nice to her. And I cried 'cause she said I was stupid to be nice—that I never get anything from it."

"I'm so sorry she said that, Mikey. She was wrong."

"Well, Miss Rosie, I know she was wrong. That's why I was cryin'. I feel real sorry for her. I want her to know what it's like to be loved, like I know I'm loved. I know Jesus, He loves me, and my Heavenly Father, He loves me, too, 'cause my parents, they tell me so. Maybe no one ever loved Gertrude like that, so she doesn't know how to accept God's love."

"Wow, Mikey. I think you may be right," Rosie had said as she thought on what her young student had just revealed to her.

"Do ya think ya could help her? Show her God's love extra-special like, so she can understand it? Maybe then, she'll want to be like Jesus."

"That's a wonderful idea, Mikey. Will you pray for me while I undertake this God-sized task? I can't do it without His help."

"You bet I will! Thanks, Miss Rosie! 'Bye!"

That day, Rosie began to pray in great earnest in regards to her approach to Gertrude. And little by little, God answered the prayers of Mikey and her. Rosie was firm with Gertrude, but she always disciplined in an attitude of love. She spent extra time with her wayward student and went out of her way to show her that she was interested in what Gertrude was interested in. In addition to Rosie's love, Mikey continued to be kind to Gertrude. In time, Gertrude had softened. She even earned a new nickname that Rosie had given her herself. She was now known lovingly as "Gerty" by the whole class, and she was best buddies with Mikey. She was his champion, for she admired Mikey greatly and would never forget the one who had tirelessly been kind to her, regardless of her barbs and needles.

Rosie was so thankful for her students! She went through the list of all of the children in her class and saw every face. She prayed for them all by name as she continued to gaze upon the vast night sky, filled with stars.

Then, all of a sudden, a solution to her quandary of the gifts for Christmas occurred to her. "That's it!" She said, as she turned around and rushed back down the country lane to her little house next to the school. "I'll make them each their own little star! I'll sew them together out of some scrap pieces of cloth! And I'll include a little note with each one."

Once Rosie arrived at her home, she opened the door and shut it quickly behind her. She lit a lantern and took off her wrap. She went over to her desk, and taking a seat, she took up pencil and paper and began to write the following:

My dear pupil,

Merry Christmas! Have you ever stared out at the night sky and noticed the stars? There are so many that we can't even number them! But you know what? God knows how many stars there are.

There are so many stars that we can't even see them all. But God sees them. He calls each of them by name.

You are like one of God's stars. You may feel small sometimes and like one among many in the vast sky, but guess what? God knows you, and He made you to shine the light that only you can shine and to be the blessing that only you can be. So draw near to Him—for He is the source of your light—and never let your light go out!

Thank you for being such a blessing to me. I love you and Merry Christmas!

Love,

Your Teacher,

Miss Rosie

Rosie sat back in her chair and smiled. "Thank You, dear Lord! Your creativity is endless and Your Love, Never-ending. Thank You for loving me and all of the little children you have entrusted to my care. You are a great God and there is none like You. Help me to give them the love that they need, the love that comes from You."

As Rosie rose from her desk, she began to hum a hymn of praise and get ready for bed. As she closed her eyes in sleep that night, she did so with a smile on her face in anticipation of a joyful Christmas season full of celebrating her Lord's birth, and a heart full of hope for what the Lord had planned for her and her students in the coming year.

"Good night, dear Lord," Rosie whispered as she drifted off to a sweet and restful night's sleep.

~Psalm 147:4~

A Special Note:

This story is dedicated to my Grandma who was affectionately known as "Rosie" in her youth, as I

mentioned at the end of an earlier story. She became a schoolteacher when she graduated from college. The first school that she taught in was a one-room schoolhouse in Illinois in the late 1930's. She walked two miles to the school every day and was responsible for starting the fire in the school stove and keeping it going throughout the day. I used to love hearing the stories she told me about her life. Though she is in heaven now, her memory is still held very dear in my heart. Grandma, this story is for you.

Day 15:

Joshua's Christmas Gift

It was Christmas time again, and just like every year, Emily decorated her home and went shopping for gifts. She also continued to go to church every Sunday and Wednesday, volunteering in the children's ministry every Sunday morning. She loved the kids, and the kids loved her.

Emily had a busy life. She had filled it to the brim with responsibilities and tasks of all kinds. She worked during the week at a department store in the local mall where she had been employed for the past five years.

Christmas was the busiest time of the year for Emily at work. By the time she made it to church at the end of the week, she was hard-pressed to find the energy to work with the eager seven year-olds in her care.

After one especially rough week, filled with Christmas sales and complaining customers, Emily arrived at church completely deflated. Her goal was to get through the morning and go home and rest, so she could be ready for the next harrowing week—the week before Christmas.

Emily made it through to the end of the Sunday school class, then dismissed the children to the great room where they could mill around, have cookies and juice, and wait for their parents to come and pick them up after the church service. While she was cleaning up, she looked up and noticed that one of the boys had not left yet. He was sitting at the back of the room, engrossed in one of the Bible story lesson books full of pictures and simple words.

"Joshua," Emily said gently. She had a soft spot for this sweet-natured boy with a heart of gold. "What are you up to? Your parents will be looking for you soon."

"Will you tell me this story again, Miss Emily— the one about the shepherds and the baby Jesus? It's my favorite," Joshua asked expectantly.

"Of course," Emily answered. She was tired, but she could not turn down such a request. So she began, "When Mary had baby Jesus, she and Joseph were in Bethlehem. They had traveled there from their own town, but there was no room for them in the inn at the time of Jesus' birth, so they had to wrap Jesus in cloths and lay Him in a manger—a feeding trough for animals. In that same area, at the time Jesus was born, there were shepherds watching their flocks of sheep in the field at night when the angel of the Lord appeared to them and God's glory shined on them. And they were very afraid."

Emily stopped speaking for a moment so that she could open her Bible to chapter two of the book of Luke. She then read, "Then the angel said to them, 'Do not be afraid, for behold, I bring you good tidings of great joy which will be to all people. For there is born to you this day in the city of David a Savior, who is Christ the Lord. And this will be the sign to you: You will find a Babe wrapped in swaddling cloths, lying in a manger.' And suddenly there was with the angel a multitude of the heavenly host praising God and saying: 'Glory to God in the highest, and on earth peace, goodwill toward men!'" (Luke 2:10-14)

As Emily looked up from her reading, she turned back to Joshua and continued the story, "And the shepherds went into the town of Bethlehem right away and found baby Jesus with Mary and Joseph— and He was lying in a manger just as the angel had said. After they had seen Him, they went away telling people everywhere the good news that the angel had told them about this wonderful new baby. And the Bible says, 'But Mary kept all these things and pondered them in her heart,'" Emily said as she finished the story (Luke 2:19).

"Wow," Joshua said softly. He seemed in a state of awe. After a long pause of silence which Emily was hesitant to break, Joshua looked up at her and said, "I'm so happy about Christmas, Miss Emily. Jesus is the best gift ever! And I have Him every day all year long. Isn't God so wonderful to give us Christmas?"

For a moment, Emily sat speechless. She knew that Joshua's family was going through a hard time right now. They were very tight on funds, and there were three children in the family. They could not afford a fancy Christmas this year just like so many others in the congregation. Yet this young boy was full of thankfulness and praise for his Heavenly Father who had given him his wonderful Savior and Best Friend, Jesus. He was enjoying Christmas and Joshua's sweet sincerity had a strong effect on Emily's heart.

After another pause, Emily swallowed past the lump in her throat and said with tears in her eyes, "Yes, Joshua. God is truly wonderful, and your Christmas gift is the best gift there is. Let's pray that you will always know such joy and peace form knowing our Lord and Savior, Jesus Christ."

As they prayed quietly together, Emily's heart became calm. A short time later, Joshua's family came looking for him. It was time for him to go home. Emily decided to stay in the Sunday school room for some time that afternoon to pray.

"Dear Heavenly Father," she prayed, "You know me, and You know how much I needed to hear what Joshua said today. I have been so busy that I have been dreading every day of this season. Forgive me, Father. Your gift of love—Your Son, Jesus—is my reason to rejoice always. He is Joshua's gift this Christmas and all year long—just as He is mine and every believer's. You are so awesome and holy, Lord. Please use me this Christmas to share Your Gift of Love with others. Thank You, Lord—thank You for Your Truth—thank You for Jesus! In Jesus' Name, Amen."

When Emily arrived at her apartment later that day, she spent the rest of the day in the Word of God and in some much-needed prayer with her Heavenly Father. She delighted in the joy of just being in the presence of God. She had some catching up to do, and she decided that today was just the day to do it. It looked like it would be a beautiful Christmas, after all!

Day 16:

Luke 2:1–20

"And it came to pass in those days *that* a decree went out from Caesar Augustus that all the world should be registered. This census first took place while Quirinius was governing Syria. So all went to be registered, everyone to his own city.

Joseph also went up from Galilee, out of the city of Nazareth, into Judea, to the city of David, which is called Bethlehem, because he was of the house and lineage of David, to be registered with Mary, his betrothed wife,

who was with child. So it was, that while they were there, the days were completed for her to be delivered. And she brought forth her firstborn Son, and wrapped Him in swaddling cloths, and laid Him in a manger, because there was no room for them in the inn.

Now there were in the same country shepherds living out in the fields, keeping watch over their flock by night. And behold, an angel of the Lord stood before them, and the glory of the Lord shone around them, and they were greatly afraid. Then the angel said to them, 'Do not be afraid, for behold, I bring you good tidings of great joy which will be to all people. For there is born to you this day in the city of David a Savior, who is Christ the Lord. And this *will* be the sign to you: You will find a Babe wrapped in swaddling cloths, lying in a manger.'

And suddenly there was with the angel a multitude of the heavenly host praising God and saying:

'Glory to God in the highest,

And on earth peace, goodwill toward men!'

So it was, when the angels had gone away from them into heaven, that the shepherds said to one another, 'Let us now go to Bethlehem and see this thing that has come to pass, which the Lord has made known to us.'

And they came with haste and found Mary and Joseph, and the Babe lying in a manger. Now when they had seen *Him*, they made widely known the saying which was told them concerning this Child. And all those who heard *it* marveled at those things which were told them by the shepherds. But Mary kept all these things and pondered *them* in her heart. Then the shepherds returned, glorifying and praising God for all the things that they had heard and seen, as it was told them."

Day 17:

Bethlehem's Old Woodcarver

Let me tell you an amazing story of how God took one man's tragedy and turned it into beautiful, hand-carved offerings of love that blessed a whole town. There is an old woodcarver by the name of Nathan who lives on the outskirts of modern-day Bethlehem. He is a simple man, but the wisdom he possesses is rare.

One Spring, several years ago, Nathan lost his wife to a bombing in downtown Bethlehem. It crushed him, and he thought that he would never recover. His whole life was gone, for she was all that was good in his life, and since his retirement, she had meant more to him than ever. His loss caused him to turn to God in fury. He figured that he no longer had anything to lose, so why not be fearless in his approach? He was a religious Jew and a faithful one, but he was beyond the point of paying heed to religion.

He asked God questions, and he demanded answers. He wanted to know why sweet and beautiful people had to die when it was others who were twisted with cruelty and hate. He wanted to know why

Israel seemed to be chosen for suffering above all else. But most of all, he wanted to know where the promised Savior was. He knew that his people had been waiting on the Messiah for thousands of years, and he figured that now would be a pretty nice time for Him to come. Nathan forgot his fear of God in his anger and hurt. He could only see one thing: his pain.

The one thing that Nathan did right was to go to God. Nathan gave God an ultimatum, if you can picture a *human* giving God an ultimatum. He let God know that he would give Him one last opportunity to make things clear. Nathan decided to go to the ancient scriptures and seek God. He decided that he could no longer listen only to the words of a rabbi. He needed a word from God Himself. What he found changed his life.

Nathan searched the scriptures tirelessly for answers. He wanted so much to be comforted. One day, Nathan was reading in Isaiah 7:14 about the coming Savior being born of a virgin, and something came to mind. He flipped to Micah 5:2 and read of the coming Savior being born in Bethlehem. His mind was then filled with memories of nativities from Christmases past in his town of Bethlehem, and he wondered if it was at all possible that the promised Messiah had already come. He had to know.

So, Nathan went to a bookstore in town that summer day and bought his very first Bible. He was familiar with most of what was called the "Old Testament," but the "New Testament" was another story altogether. He read it from cover to cover, searching for answers. Then he came back to the book of John. He was touched by this Jesus. He had never known of anyone like Him. He found himself believing that

Jesus really is the Son of God. He was in a state of complete wonder. God had already sent the Messiah. He came 2000 years ago in the form of a carpenter named Jesus. And the reason He came was to die and be raised back to life again for lost ones like Nathan, so they can make their way into the arms of the Father.

Nathan was shaken to his very core. That summer, amidst tragedy, he met His Savior, Jesus Christ, on his knees in prayer. He was overtaken by the first true sense of peace he had ever known. He knew that He was loved and that God was right there with him and would never leave his side. There was a lot that he did not yet understand. But he was willing to trust the One who had laid His life down so that Nathan could know this new life and true love.

This awesome revelation touched Nathan so deeply that he felt a need to respond. He was filled with love for His Savior, so he expressed it in the only way he knew how. He began to carve.

Nathan had owned a woodcarving shop before his retirement, and he was known all over Bethlehem for his fine workmanship. He was one of the true artisans of his time, and the furniture made by his hand was highly valued. When he retired, he had put aside some very fine olive wood, intending to use it to make a new set of furniture as an anniversary gift to his wife.

On one of the first days after her death, he had taken an axe in his fury and chopped the wood to bits.

Nathan now went back to his workshop and used that same wood to begin a new labor of love. Every day he went and sat carving and praying. The carvings he made were all related to Jesus. Most of them were related to His birth, since Nathan had first come to Jesus by memories of nativity scenes. He also carved some crosses as reminders that His sins were forgiven and that he was welcome to come to the Heavenly Father with all of his cares.

As the months went by, Nathan continued to carve. He had made hundreds of carvings by now. He had no reason for carving them. He simply felt that they somehow touched God's heart, and that in-turn blessed Nathan.

December came, and the bombings in Bethlehem had escalated. Nathan's heart went out to the families of the victims, and he prayed for them all as he sat carving in his workshop. Because of all of the violence, the government announced that Christmas would not be celebrated that year.

Nathan did not understand why this fighting and destruction had to take place, so he went to his knees in prayer. He asked God to use him to bless others that year in a way that would give them the peace that he had been blessed with. He knew that he could do nothing to change the state of the world. It was possible, however, for him to point his neighbors in the direction of the truth that leads to true peace. God showed him how he could accomplish this.

It all became so clear to him! There was a purpose and, more specifically, a person for every one of those carvings. God would use Nathans's simple gift from his heart to bless hundreds. The carvings would remind some, and introduce others, to the fact that Christmas is about Jesus, and its celebration can never be cancelled when He lives in your heart.

This was the plan that Nathan followed. He gave each of his friends, neighbors, old customers, acquaintances, and many others a carving along with a Merry Christmas letter. He received many odd glances and a few open-mouthed stares from those who had known him to be a devout follower of Judaism and its traditions. He just smiled back at them in his quiet way, told them about Jesus, and asked them if they had any special needs that they would like for him to pray for.

He also let each one of them know that his workshop, although now closed to customers, was always open to anyone who wanted to drop by.

God used Nathan to touch the lives of people throughout the entire community of Bethlehem that Christmas. Tragedy had been transformed into victory in this one man's life, and the lives of hundreds were affected by it. Nathan's wisdom continued to grow as he continued to walk and talk with God. He continued to carve in his workshop, and people often came to see Nathan for advice or just for a nice chat.

Nathan is now known as Bethlehem's wise old woodcarver. His wisdom comes from his knowledge that the only true answers in life come from Jesus Christ, the Son of the living God. That wisdom began growing with his first cry of help to God.

To this very day, Nathan points everyone who comes his way straight to the hope of Jesus.

Day 18:

Nathan's Christmas Letter

Dear Friends,

Happy Hanukkah and Merry Christmas to you all.

I know that the times are hardly merry, but though it seems beyond belief, we have a wonderful reason to celebrate. I want to tell you about the One who has changed my life in a most unbelievable way this year. God has enabled me to share my heart with you, so I am opening up to you now as my true friends and my dearly loved countrymen.

Those of you who know me well know that I recently lost my wife of almost 50 years this past May to a terrorist bombing in our beloved city of Bethlehem.

There was no life for me when she died. I knew no hope. For me, life had left the earth when she died. I went into isolation and asked God why He had chosen the people of Israel for such misery. I asked Him why such beautiful people must die, all because of the ugly and cruel hatred of others.

I could find no answers. I began to question whether God really did exist, and I wondered how He could stay silent to the cries of His people for so long. I did not understand. So, I gave God an ultimatum. I would search for answers one last time in His holy scriptures. If I did not find reason enough to give my devotion to Him, then I would discard all of my age-old beliefs and traditions. What good would they do me if they were only words? I needed more than the word of the rabbi. I needed a Word from God.

How I cringe now as I look back and think how easy it would have been for God to have remained silent... Praise God for His wondrous mercy to answer the "ultimatum" of one so very small.

But God did not remain silent. No. Rather, He opened my eyes to a truth I had never known. He introduced me to His Son, Jesus. I wept when I met him, for I saw immediately the futility of my plight. I was a man, created by God, but forever separated from Him and doomed to death ever since Adam took that first bite of apple. I was a sinner, and I was ashamed. But God called me to Him, being ever merciful and ever loving. He introduced me to grace in the form of His Son. And, yes, I am saying that Jesus is the Son of God.

Friends, rejoice! Our long-awaited Messiah has come! He came 2000 years ago, and He was born here in our town—the town of Bethlehem! Just as our ancestors rejected Him years ago, so too do we. Let us open our hearts to Him and give our Lord the only gift He wants: ourselves.

Open your heart and accept the gift of love and forgiveness that will change your heart. My Lord Jesus has transformed me and forever changed my life. I will never pass through another day that I do not ache for my wife, Gladys, but I now know a love deeper than I ever shared with her. The love I shared with her grew over many years, just as this love with my Savior is growing in me now day by day as I share every step of my life with Him. He is my love, and He sustains me.

This is just my story, and I know that you all have similar ones. But is Jesus the One you run to for help and healing? Because I can guarantee that if He is not, you are not experiencing true life, and you never will unless you come to Him and accept His offering of love. I cannot do anything to stop the bombings that are happening all around us, and I cannot cause the government to change its decision to cancel the celebration of Christmas, but I can share the story of Christmas with you.

Ever since I first came to know Jesus, I have been in awe of His humble birth. I keep coming back to it, and I cannot stop thinking about it. You all know how I love to carve. My old woodcarving shop was not only my living but also my passion. In some way as I work with my hands, I am able to express the feelings that I have inside. When I retired, I had put away some very fine olive wood to carve a new set of furniture for Gladys for our 50th Anniversary. I hacked the wood into bits in one of the first angry days after her death. There is a point to this, my dear friends. They are not the mere ramblings of an old man's decrepit mind—not yet at any rate and God willing, not ever—but back to the point.

After God showed me the truth of His Son, Jesus Christ, I began to carve nativity scenes and crosses, putting all of my passion into the work. I used the wood that I had intended to bless Gladys with, and I carved in every spare minute that I had. The carving kept my mind focused on my Lord, and it helped to take my mind off of my loss. I worked hard, and I prayed as I worked. I prayed for our people and for others like me who had lost so much. I prayed for healing and revelation, and I prayed that our nation would be restored to our God in the name of His Son, Jesus Christ. I prayed for you all, my friends. I prayed that you would know the same peace, healing, and even joy that God has shown me in these hard times. It is what I desire for you all.

The way to find this life and to know this love is simple. You must first admit to God that you are a sinner and that no matter what you do, you will never be able to be good enough to come to Him and make it to heaven in your own power. Admit that you need His help. God wants you to know that He loves you. His proof is that He sent His only Son who is precious, blameless, and holy, into the world, stripped of all glory. He sent Him as a baby, the Son of God, born here in our very city of Bethlehem. He grew up in the house of a humble carpenter. God sent Him to earth to live among those who did not recognize Him for who He was. He is the One by whom and through whom the world was made. He knows all. But they did not recognize Him. They killed Him and mocked Him, but He did nothing wrong. He was completely blameless.

That was not the end, though. He was raised to life again on the third day after His crucifixion—and He conquered the power of sin and death and made the way for us to get to God the Father. Just as sin entered the world through one, our sins can be forgiven if we accept the One who died for them (Romans 5:12-21). Jesus never sinned, so His death and His act of love is able to cover all of our sins. He is an entirely blameless offering—pure and holy and completely acceptable to God. His sacrifice meets all of God's requirements for our sins to be covered and wiped away forever (1 Peter 1:18-19).

God has made it easy on you, my friends. All you need to do is come to Him and ask for His forgiveness. Submit to Him as your King and give your life to Him. He can do so much more with your life than you can—and for the first time you will experience true joy and peace. Joy and peace are not feelings that fade. When you know Jesus, they are promises that are yours when you live in the power of the Holy Spirit.

Finally, my friends, my Christmas prayer is not world peace—for this world will never know peace for as long as it rejects its Maker. No—my desire is that you as individuals will know the truth of God— for I know that His truth will enable you to truly experience peace, joy, love, and life to the fullest no matter what circumstance you find yourself in.

I am giving each of you a carving to do with as you wish. I hope that it will be a blessing to you and point you toward your Maker. May God bless you, my friends, as you celebrate Hanukkah—and Merry Christmas to you all!

Your Friend and Bethlehem's Old Woodcarver,

Nathan

Day 19:

A Walk with the God Who Made the Stars

I went for a walk tonight. The night was so sill, and the air was so crisp as I took a winter stroll with myCreator.

December is such a beautiful time of year, don't you think? But things can get hurried and crazy if you aren't careful, and that is exactly why I needed this time alone with my Best Friend and Lord, Jesus Christ. I needed to re-center my focus so that it remained on Him, where it was supposed to be, instead of shifting to the many distractions in my life that were clamoring to be number one.

So I took a walk in the winter night air to clearmy head and just be with my Creator, who knows mebetter than I know myself.

My name is Cassandra Woodruff, and I love Christmas! I love the nights of Christmas most of all, I think—when families cozy up together by the Christmas tree to watch Christmas specials—or play games—or my favorite!—to listen to the story of the birth of Jesus Christ, who is the most Amazing gift ever given.

I often take long winter walks at night to get away from all of the activity for a while, so I can be with the One who Christmas is supposed to be all about.

It can be so easy to lose focus of my Lord in all of the busyness of such a wonderful season, and I just don't want to miss a single day of living to know my Lord Jesus more deeply and walking with Him more closely by staying connected to Him in prayer throughout the day and listening for the gentle whisper of His Holy Spirit as He leads me day by day.

So tonight as I took such a walk, taking in the sights of the lovely Christmas lights in my neighborhood, I sked God to speak to my heart and remind me of His goodness and how Mighty He is.

As I was walking in the stillness of the night, noticing the puffs of my breath in the frigid air, God drew my attention to the sky.

Oh, it was such a beautiful night! There was no moon, and the sky was absolutely studded with stars!

As I looked, I felt God speak to my heart:

"Cassandra, do you see those stars? I made them for you. I knew when I created them that you would be walking on this night and would look up and be in wonder of how Great I Am. I love you, Cassandra. I love you more than you can fathom. I love that you have a childlike heart and a childlike faith, and I love that you come to Me with absolute trust in My goodness. I love you.

"Share My love with others this season and into the New Year. I know that you are shy of mentioning Me when you are talking to others that don't know Me and even those who do know Me.

"Don't be afraid. Tell of My goodness. Tell of My Love. Tell of your relationship with Me. Sprinkle your speech with the salt of My Light, My Truth, and My Love.

"I will bless such conversation, and I will bless you when you speak of Me to others with a pure heart.

"Be quick to listen for my voice, and be slow to speak—but when you do speak, ask Me to speak through you by My Holy Spirit who is within you.

"I love you, Cassandra! Enjoy every day of your Merry Christmas in Me!"

As I listened, my heart swelled with love for the Lover of my Soul—my Redeemer and Best Friend—my Lord, Jesus Christ and God, my Heavenly Father.

I felt so completely washed over with Love and joy—peace and fullness in my Lord Jesus Christ.

I walked on, just being still in the presence of my Maker and rejoicing in my spirit over this love and intimacy that He has blessed me to share with Him.

And then it hit me!

This love—this intimacy—He wanted me to share it with others, that they too may know Him in such a way if they choose to confess Jesus Christ as Lord with their mouths and believe in their hearts that God raised Jesus from the dead (Romans 10:9-13).

God wants me to testify to how Good He is. I am a personal, first-hand witness of the goodness of God, and He wants my life to overflow with that love which He washes me and fills me with every time that I am in His presence. He also longs for my speech to be sprinkled with testimonies of how good He is—and especially how good He has been to me.

Such a life draws seekers to the Lord—for how can they know the Lord unless they hear about Him— and who better to tell about Him than someone who knows Him personally? (Romans 10:14-15)

As I turned the corner that led me back to my house, I realized how very Good God is! Such an Awesome Creator, He is Bigger than we can imagine— yet He longs to be in intimate relationships with the people He made in His image—us—all mankind.

How Mighty He is—the Maker of the stars! And how Good He is! There is no one like Him!

No one else is truly Good—only God. Only God sent His holy, perfect Son, Jesus, who was with Him before the beginning of time and who is God Himself (John 1:1)—to earth as a baby to live, bring us the good news of salvation, die, and be raised to life in three days so that we may have eternal life and victory over sin and death as we believe in and follow Him in obedience and submission to His Holy Spirit. How Very good God is!

When I arrived at my doorstep, I turned around and took one last look up at the stars as I breathed a prayer,

> *"O Lord, how beautiful the stars are! And Your Word says You know them each by name! (Psalm 147:4)*

> *"Thank You for Your Goodness! Thank You for Your Greatness! Thank You for Your Love! And thank You for Your Might.*

> *"I love You, Lord! Bless me now as I go in, and make me a blessing to my family for the rest of the night. Oh, how I need You, Lord—every moment! Thank You that You welcome me to draw near to You, and You always want to see me and be near me—even after I have done wrong. Once I confess my wrongdoing, you always wash me, cleanse me, and bless me with Your beautiful presence anew.*

> *"Oh, Lord! I love You! "In Jesus' Name, Amen!"*

As I walked into the house, my quiet time with the Lord ended, but He did not stay outside. He came with me, for Jesus never leaves me or forsakes me—He is always by my side. I had refueled and refocused and was now ready to resume my family role.

It is so comforting to know that the God who made the stars loves me dearly. He loves me and all the people in the world so much that He gave the most He could possibly give—His holy Son's life—for the redemption of our sinful selves—that our sin may be covered by Jesus' shed blood and washed away, making us whiter than snow in God's eyes. God wants us to know Him personally as our Heavenly Father through belief in His Son, Jesus, and He also wants us to be saved from the destruction of His wrath—which we deserve for the many sins we have committed.

A right, beautiful, and intimate relationship with God could never have been possible for anyone without the sacrificial gift of Jesus Christ, God's holy Son. We just can never be good enough in ourselves to make the requirements to come near to a perfect, holy, sovereign King and God. God loves us so very much to do what we could never do so that we could know Him in such an intimate way! Oh, He truly does love us!

Oh, how Good He is, and I am now ready to share the good news of His Amazing Love through my life and my words as He leads.

Oh, God is so Good! Merry Christmas!

And this year, may you celebrate His Life and Love along with me!

In Jesus' Name, May it be so! Amen.

~Cassandra Woodruff~

Day 20:

Some Thoughts on Who Made the Stars

Do you believe that God made the stars?

It occurred to me as I wrote Cassandra's story about her nighttime Christmas walk with God, that many people—well, probably MOST people today— don't even believe anymore that God made the stars.

If you are one such person—Christian or no— please give me a few moments of your time.

If you do believe that Jesus is the Creator (John 1:1), I am so glad. These words are for you, too, for they are simply some thoughts of what has been stolen from us by the devil and how we can fight back God's way.

When the theory of evolution came on the scene so many years ago, a lie was told that stole more than it originally let on.

I could go on and on about what it has stolen, but I want to focus instead on one particularly Huge thing that it has stolen from people who have an ache inside of them that they cannot define.

Evolution does away with the ultimate need for God.

It is true that many who believe that life originated through natural processes also believe in God.

However, if you are one of those people, I would urge you to examine your faith—for how can you place your trust in a God who lies?

If God is God, if God is truly good, and if God can be wholly trusted, then He cannot be a liar, and His Word should, therefore, be absolutely true (Titus 1:2). If God truly is God, then He should never make mistakes, be all knowing, and 100% perfect.

Otherwise, how could He be called "God"?

If God IS perfect and trustworthy and good and unable to lie, then His Word MUST be true—ALL of it.

If that is not who God is, then who is He? Either God is or God is not.

That is all there can be.

If God is, then we cannot define Him.

He defines Himself, and He has done that for us in His Word, the Bible, and in the evidence of His touch on all that He has created.

(Romans 1:20)

The Bible is either the truth or it is a bunch of lies.

A fact is either true or it is not. It is not optional. It either is or it is not. Whether one believes a fact does not change whether it is true. It just changes how you view reality.

So it is with God and the truth of His Word.

You see, if God didn't make the stars, and God didn't make the earth, and God didn't make all life on earth, then didn't make us.

And if God didn't make us, then we never sinned against Him, we don't need a Savior, and we will never know Him personally or live with Him forever— because He doesn't even exist!

How convenient all of this is for the devil—who is the true father of all lies (John 8:44)—because if God doesn't exist, then the devil doesn't exist either, and he can do whatever God allows him to do (Job 1:6-12) without people knowing it was him!

Do you see the danger of the deception of evolution?

It removes the need for a Creator, ultimately removing your need for Jesus.

God loves you, and Oh, how He wants to know you intimately! He longs for you to draw near to Him, that He may uncover His heart to you.

Don't rob yourself or allow yourself to be robbed of the most intimate relationship you can ever have.

For only those who live to know Jesus have that hole within them filled, and are able to experience true joy forevermore.

I encourage you this Christmas to look up at the night sky and ask yourself this question, "Who or what made the stars? Was it God or a natural occurrence?" What you believe is more significant than you may know.

For only those who believe in God as their Creator can fully experience the Awe and Wonder of His Love for all mankind—the ones He has made in His own image, uniquely individual, and fashioned with His very hands (Genesis 1:27; Psalm 139:13-16).

He made us in His own image and blessed us. If we don't believe that, and we don't believe man and woman ever sinned in the Garden of Eden, then why would we believe that we need a Savior to redeem us from our sins?

That line of reasoning doesn't make much sense. Jesus would then just have been an eccentric man who lived long ago that people happened to place their faith and trust in.

But what Jesus said, and the reason He supposedly came, could not possibly be true if you don't believe that God created the world.

Does that make sense?

So, I leave you with this as we celebrate Christmas this year.

Who is Jesus to you?

Is He just a cute baby in a manger scene?

Is He a historical figure that lived a long time ago and was put to death on a Roman cross?

Or is He the God who came to save you from your sins?

Is He the God who made a way for you to live abundantly every day with Him and live forever with Him one day in heaven when He was raised from death to life by God on the third day after He died?

And finally, is Jesus your Creator—the One who existed in the beginning with God and the One who IS God?

Who is Jesus to you?

Live to know the One who knows you and loves you more than you can imagine.

You will never exhaust the depths of His love or reach the end of all there is to know in your relationship with Him—for He is infinite.

Merry Christmas!

And may you be truly blessed in the knowledge and grace and power of our Lord Jesus Christ as you place your trust and hope completely in Him!

In Jesus' Name, Amen.

Day 21:

Christmas in Harmony with Jesus

The Christmas tree is up.

Carols are being sung.

But have we forgotten

The most important One?

This is mentioned a lot

At this time of year.

Christmas is Jesus' birthday.

But in our hearts is this clear?

We may hear in church

That Christmas is about Christ,

But in our hearts do we honor Him,

Trusting and obeying Him no matter our plight?

This is a challenge for me

In the hustle and bustle of life,

To slow down and be still

And remember my Lord Jesus Christ.

You see, life for the Christian

Is not all doing good no matter what.

It is about a relationship,

Walking through life with Jesus even when things get tough.

Life with Jesus

Is a beautiful song

When all is in harmony

In your walk with Him the whole day long.

When you talk to Him through the day

And listen for His voice,

When you live in sweet surrender

To His love by your own choice.

When you choose to slow down

And simply be still,

Knowing that Jesus is Lord

And you are fully surrendered to His will.

Living this way

Is the sweetest of songs

Full of love for the Savior,

A Christmas gift to God that belongs

In heaven and on earth

Between child of God and Lord.

It is a song of sweet harmony.

Sung in one accord.

For it is when the child of God

Aligns his or her life with God's will

That true harmony, peace, and joy are experienced

To the heart's fill.

O blessed child of God,

Let us rejoice this Christmas time!

And let us slow down, too

And love God with all our heart, our soul, our mind.

In Jesus' Name, May it be so!

May we connect with Jesus today!

He is only

A simple prayer away!

Day 22:

Winter Majesty
A Christmas Song

(Verse 1)

Snowflakes floating through the sky…

Skaters flowing gracefully by.

Beauty dances in the air,

All is joyful, calm, and clear.

(Chorus 1)

I have you,

You have me,

Here in this wondrous mystery.

We are together,

And we have love.

What great blessings from Up Above!

(Verse 2)

Bare branches all around.

We find a bench, and sit down.

You put your hand sweetly in mine,

All is peaceful, all is right.

(Chorus 1)

I have you,

You have me,

Here in this wondrous mystery.

We are together,

And we have love.

What great blessings from Up Above!

(Verse 3)

When finally it's time to go,

We rise again, we take it slow.

We walk in step, side by side,

Full of the wonder of this night.

(Chorus 2)

I have you,

You have me.

Here in this wondrous mystery.

We are together,

And we have love.

We have our Father up above.

(Verse 4)

All is peaceful, calm, and bright.

We are precious in His sight.

He has painted this beautiful night.

His Winter Majesty brought to light.

(Bridge)

Thank You,

For giving us this time.

Lord, we Praise You,

For giving us Your Love.

It's all because of You.

Lord, it's all because of You.

We give glory and honor to You,

For we can say:

(Chorus 1)

I have you,

You have me,

Here in this wondrous mystery.

We are together,

And we have love.

What great blessings from Up Above!

(Chorus 3)

I have you,

You have me,

Here in this wondrous mystery!

We are together,

And we have love.

Thank You, Father, for Your Love.

Thank You, Father, for Your Love.

Day 23:

Jenny and Paco's First Christmas

"Here, Paco! Come here, boy!" Jenny called to her adorable pug puppy. Paco snorted excitedly as hetrotted over to Jenny's couching form.

"Today is my first day of Christmas vacation, Paco, and we have lots to do! There are Christmas presents to wrap, Christmas cookies to eat, and

Christmas specials to watch! Let's get started!"

"Ruff! Ruff!" Paco barked. He was just as excited as Jenny, because being with her was his favorite occupation.

"Alright… first on the list is wrapping the

Christmas presents! Let's get some Christmas paper out, Paco!" Jenny said.

"Ruff!" Paco replied. His paws padded on the floor as he followed closely behind Jenny.

"Now let's see," Jenny thought aloud, "We'll need paper, scissors, tape, bows, tags, and pens to write on the tags. Oh! And one more thing! Let's put on some Christmas music, too!" Jenny said energetically as she danced over to select her favorite music.

Paco wagged his little curly tail back and forth. His small pink tongue was hanging out of his mouth, and he was as happy as could be. This Christmas thing was fun stuff! As Jenny wrapped presents and hummed along to her favorite Christmas tunes, Paco trotted here, there and all around her, helping out where he could and making Jenny laugh. They were a great team.

When Jenny and Paco were finished wrapping Christmas presents, Jenny positioned them underneath the beautiful tree. Paco continued to help out by nudging the presents further into place with his scrunched up little nose.

"Wasn't that fun, Paco?"

"Ruff! Ruff!" Paco jumped at Jenny's legs and Jenny reached down to scoop him up into her arms. She gave him a kiss and brought him close to her face, so he could give her lots of kisses, too.

"I love you, Paco!" Jenny said as she hugged Paco close.

"Rrruff!" Paco replied with great enthusiasm.

"Now for some cookies! You want a treat boy?" Jenny asked in a tone that Paco knew well.

"Yip! Yip!" Paco started wriggling so much and getting so excited that Jenny laughed and set him down.

"Alright," Jenny smiled, "Christmas cookies for me and special treats for you."

Paco was beside himself with excitement! He was barking and jumping and barking some more. He LOVED treats!

Jenny went to the kitchen with Paco close on her heels. She went to the cabinet where she kept Paco's teats and took one out.

"Alright. Sit up, boy."

Paco happily obeyed, and Jenny tossed him the treat.

"Good boy!" she said as Paco jumped up and caught the treat in mid-air. As he was crunching away on his little biscuit, Jenny found the sugar cookies that her mother had baked.

"Oh, look, Paco! These cookies are just beautiful!

I bet they're yummy, too. I think I'll take this red bell and the green tree, and I'll get some milk, too."

Paco was quite busy at the moment with his treat, so he did not reply. But Jenny did not mind in the least. She was having the greatest day! She put her two cookies on a Christmas plate, poured herself a giant glass of ice-cold milk, and settled down at the kitchen table.

When Paco was finished eating his treat, he ran excitedly to Jenny's side to see if she had anything else for him. Jenny laughed and said, "Okay, boy. Just this once. Since it's Christmas time, I'll give you another one."

"Ruff! Ruff!" Paco barked and wagged his adorable tail. He was quite pleased. When Jenny gave him his second treat, he ate it happily. When he was finished, he settled down at Jenny's feet and waited for her to finish her snack.

As Jenny was cleaning up, she said, "Are you ready to watch a Christmas special, Paco?"

"Ruff!" Paco replied. He did not know what was coming next, but as long as he was with Jenny, he knew that he would like it.

"We are going to watch a special about Jesus being born!" Jenny said as they moved into the family room.

Once they were all settled in and watching the Christmas special, Jenny gave Paco a big squeeze and said, "I love you, Paco! What a great first day of vacation! I'll never forget it!"

But Paco did not respond this time. He was sound asleep, snoring happily as he dreamed of his wonderful day with Jenny.

Day 24:

Oscar the Christmas Puppy

Oscar the puppy loved everything about Christmas.

He loved trotting about in the powdery Christmas snow with his red Santa hat on.

He loved catching Christmas snowflakes on his tongue.

He loved that each person in his family had a special sparkle in their eye.

He loved the fun music that made him want to dance and the special music that sent shivers up and down hisspine.

He loved all of the yummy treats there were to eat.

He loved giving gifts and getting them, too!

But most of all, Oscar loved Jesus.

Oscar knew that Jesus was the reason for Christmas.

He knew that Christmas was a celebration of Jesus' birth.

And because Oscar loved Jesus so much, that made Christmas the best time of the year.

Yes, Oscar was definitely a Christmas puppy!

Day 25:

One Starry Night

Christmas Dreams

On one starry night

Fill my heart with wonder

And with a Beautiful Light.

For deep within

A spark has been lit—

A spark of Life,

Containing peace and joy within it.

Snowflakes dance

Their way to the ground.

A silvery moon

Shines bright all around.

The snow-covered banks

Glisten in the moonlight.

The night is so still.

What a beautiful sight!

And as I dream dreams of Christmas,

The Holy Spirit reminds me—

God made all I see.

He created this Beauty.

"Thank You, Lord, for creating

This stillness that reminds me

To come before You with thanksgiving

And just simply be."

A Christmas Prayer

For You and Your Family

We have come to the end of our Christmas
stories and poems for this year.

I hope and pray that they have been a
blessing to you and your family!

Merry Christmas!

May God bless your New Year richly with His
love and a deeper relationship with Him.

May many blessings be yours as you walk with Jesus every day!

In Jesus' Name, Amen!

Knowing Jesus and God's Love

For Yourself

Do you know that God loves you? Did you know that God made you for a special reason? He loves you very much.

The Bible says that every good and perfect gift is from above—from God, the Heavenly Father (James 1:17). Can you think of some good and perfect things in your life? Those are some ways that God is showing you that He loves you.

God's biggest gift to you is Jesus. God sent His only Son Jesus to earth to live, die a cruel death on a cross, and be raised to life from the dead.

Why? Because He loves you... He wants you to know Him personally... And He wants you to live with Him forever one day.

You see, every person does wrong things, which are called sin, and deserves to be punished forever—but when we receive Jesus as our Lord, our sin is forgiven, because Jesus died in our place. Jesus lived the only perfect life, and that is why He could take our place and suffer the punishment we deserve. (Romans 3:23-26)

Now that Jesus is alive in Heaven with God after being raised from the dead, Jesus offers to cover our wrongdoing, giving us the only way to heaven, the only way to come before God, and the only way to have a personal relationship with Him. (John 14:6; Colossians 3:1)

If you want to receive God's love for you through Jesus, ask God to forgive you for your sins and help you turn from the wrong you have done. (1 John 1:9; Romans 6:23)

Believe in your heart that Jesus is God's Son and that God raised Him from the dead, and acknowledge Him as Lord of your life both in your heart and before others. (Romans 10:9-11)

Be baptized in obedience to God's Word. (Acts 2:38)

By answering God's call to believe in and love Jesus, you will become God's child, God will become your Heavenly Father, and you will be saved from God's eternal punishment in hell. (Romans 8:15-17)

God's love will now be yours to live in and share with others.

As God's child, you will have His Holy Spirit living inside of you, making you able to obey God's commands. (Romans 8:2)

God commands us to love Him and love others as we love ourselves. If we love God, we will obey His commands. (1John 5:3)

God is Love. (1 John 4:8)

Is He drawing you to Himself?

Come to Him, for He made you, He knows you better than anyone else, and He loves you more than anyone else. He knows everything you have ever done wrong, and He still loves you more than anyone else ever could. He wants you to know His deep, deep love for you.

Those who come to God are called by Him (John 6:44; Acts 2:39).

Come to Him, so that you can know His Love and so that you can live your life walking closely with Someone who will never leave you. Once you are His child, He has promised to be with you always, so there will never be a reason for you to fear. (Matthew 28:20; Hebrews 13:5)

When you place your trust in Jesus, you can know that He will always be near.

Ps 136

Michelle Lores

Writes what God puts on her heart for the purpose of producing materials that build up and strengthen families in Jesus Christ.

Her desire in doing this is to bring glory to God her

Maker and Heavenly Father.

Family is very special to God,

the Heavenly Father of all believers in Christ Jesus.

Every family on earth derives its name from Him.

(Ephesians 3:14).

May God bless you with His grace, peace, and love as you believe and trust in Him and His Son, Jesus Christ.

In Jesus' Name, Amen.

Titles by

~Michelle Lores~

Inspirational Titles

Smiling with My Lord Jesus

Smiling with My Lord Jesus: Special Edition

Growing Up in the Lord: A Journey of
Discovery in the Lord Jesus Christ

A New Day: Journey into the Light

Psalms to My Creator God: In B & W

Psalms to My Creator God: Gift Edition Esther's Voice

Life's Precious Moments

Life's Precious Moments: In B & W

Life's Precious Moments: Gift Edition

Life's Precious Moments: Gift Edition in B&W

Wintry Weather Days

Wintry Weather Days: In B & W

Wintry Weather Days: Gift Edition

Wintry Weather Days: Gift Edition in B & W

Celebrating Life in All its Ups and Downs

Celebrating Life in All its Ups and Downs: In B&W

Celebrating Life in All its Ups and Downs: Gift Edition

A Brighter Day Eternity on My Mind

A Journey of Thoughtfulness with My Lord Jesus

A Journey of Thoughtfulness with My Jesus: In B&W

Out of Darkness into His Marvelous Light: Full Color Edition

Out of a Dark Place Shines Hope

25 Ornaments on My Christmas Tree:
A Gift of Love to You from Me

A Little Book of Thanks

Milestones to Grow By

Milestones to Grow By: B&W Edition

Journey to Know My Jesus: Gift Edition

Journey to Know My Jesus: In B&W Journey to Know My Jesus

Paralyzed by Fear ~ Strengthened by Faith

Out of Darkness Into His Marvelous Light

Book of SonShine Poetry for the Heart that
Loves God: Full Color Edition

Book of SonShine Poetry for the Heart that Loves God

The Daddy Spot

Starry Night: A Christmas Collection ~ The Color Edition

Starry Night: A Christmas Collection

A Reason to Give Thanks Every Day

My Mama All Things New

Seashells by the Sea: A Collection of Poems and
Photography… The Pocketsize Edition

Seashells by the Sea: A Collection of Poems andPhotography

My Living Hope ~ In B & W ~ My Living Hope

Write with God: A Journey by Journal to Better Know God

A Poetic Christmas: The Pocketsize Edition Identity

The Torn Butterfly's Wing: And Other Poems

Countdown to Christmas! : Stories, Poems,
and Songs for the 25 Days of Christmas

Christmas Dreams by the Fire A Poetic Christmas

It's All About Jesus! ~ In Full Color

So Glad God Gave Me You!

Prayer Marbles: A Prayer Journal

The Perfect Ending to a Perfect Day

Bowling with Limes in the Morning ~ In B & W ~

My Safe Place

Christmas Stories and Poems to Warm Your Heart ~ In B & W ~

The Garden by the Sea Reflections of the Light Fresh Paint!

Bowling with Limes in the Morning: A Book of Poetry
and Reflection on Rejoicing No Matter the Season

Summer Posies: Images and Rhymes of
Florida in the Summertime

Tranquil Moments in the Garden

What is the Answer?

Sweet Memories with Mama: Color Edition His Name is
Love: A Small Book of Poetry Marriage with a Mission

It's All About Jesus Springtime is Here!

Sweet Memories with Mama Poetry, Love, & Art: In B & W
A Closer Look: A Picture Book A Season for Change

Art & the Heart of God Poems and Letters for the Hurting

A Cup of SonShine for Your Day: A 31 Day Devotional

Tikvah ~ Hope's Treasure Within ~ Poetry, Love, & Art

Christmas Stories and Poems to Warm Your Heart

When the Sun Comes Out Again: A
Collection from My Heart to Yours

Children and Family Titles

Oscar the Puppy: The Puppy Who Loves
Jesus I Love Jesus! How About You?

The Book of SonShine for Kids and Families: Short Stories
for Kids and Families Who Want to Know God

Book of SonShine Children's Story Rhymes in B&W:
Children's Story Rhymes Filled with God's Light

Book of SonShine Children's Story Rhymes in Full Color:
Children's Story Rhymes Filled with God's Light

Daisy the Flying Flower Red the Dino

Katie's Travel Journal

Building Blocks: Family Stories with Valuable Life Lessons

Little Sonny Day: And Other Godly Stories in Rhyme

The Blessing of Family ~ In B&W Prayers in the Attic

Dwight's Prayer Journal: Moving Mountains
with a Little Bit of Faith

The Blessing of Family

Button Rose ~ A Little Bunny with an Unshakeable Spirit

Andie's World Pudge the Sheep

Celebrating Seasons and Holidays with
Oscar the Puppy: Color Edition

Book of SonShine Coloring Book: For Kids and Families

Branches of the Heavenly Father's Love: Stories
and Tales for Kids and Families

Godly Stories in Rhyme: For Children and Families

Celebrating Seasons and Holidays with Oscar the Puppy

Stories and Tales Filled with God's Love: For Kids and Families

Auntie Netta's Letters to Jollee and Ned
Oscar the Christmas Puppy

Oscar the Puppy Explores His World

You can find all of Michelle's books for order at:

lulu.com/shop

Just Search

Michelle Lores,

and find your favorite title!

*For an updated list of all of Michelle's books
and their descriptions, please visit:*

MichelleLoresBooks123.wordpress.com

You can reach the author at the following email address:

Godissogoodps136@gmail.com

*May God's blessings be yours every day as
you seek Him first in Every way.*

In Jesus' Precious Name, Amen.

CPSIA information can be obtained
at www.ICGtesting.com
Printed in the USA
BVHW071343141221
624009BV00008B/454

9 781638 714194